This book is dedicated to ALL my best
friends - Elisa, Kathleen, Lisa, and Mollie-
you're all wonderful!

SIMON & SCHUSTER BOOKS FOR YOUNG READERS
An imprint of Simon & Schuster Children's Publishing Division

1230 Avenue of the Americas, New York, New York, 10020
Copyright © 2011 by Marissa Moss

For information about special discounts for bulk purchases, please contact Simon & Schuster
Special Sales at 1-866-506-1949 or business@simonandschuster.com.

The Simon & Schuster Speakers Bureau can bring authors to your live event. For more
information or to book an event, contact the Simon & Schuster Speakers Bureau at
1-866-248-3049 or visit our website at www.simonspeakers.com.

A Paula Wiseman Book

Book design by Amelia   And all my
(with help from Tom Daly) ← best friends!

No fonts
or typefaces → The text for this book is hand-lettered.
were harmed   Manufactured in China, 1210 SCP
in making
this   2   4   6   8   10   9   7   5   3   1
book!   CIP data for this book is available from
             the Library of Congress

ISBN 978-1-4424-0376-5

Nadia Kurz
61 South St
Barton, CA 91010

CAT'S GAME
48¢

Amelia
564 N. Homerest
Oopa, Oregon
97881

Whenever I get a letter from Nadia, my old best friend before I moved away, it's like finding treasure in the mailbox. Sure, we email and instant message and post stuff on Facebook, but there's NOTHING like the excitement of holding a good, old-fashioned letter in my hands. For one thing, sometimes Nadia draws pictures. For another, her handwriting is like her voice — it tells me a lot about how she's feeling. Those aren't the kind of things a computer screen can show you.

Trust me, nothing can replace a letter!

I mean, who doesn't like to get mail?

Today's letter was extra, EXTRA, <u>EXTRA</u> special!
Nadia said she's coming to visit — <u>for one whole week!</u>
Her spring break isn't the same as mine, but her mom
said she can come stay with me and even go to school
with me.

IT'S GOING TO BE GREAT!!!

Nadia and I have been best friends for a long
time — like practically forever! We used to do
everything together. Trick-or-treating, sleepovers,
birthday parties, summer camp. Then I moved away.
But we've stayed friends thanks to the power of
letters, the occasional phone call, plus a visit every
now and then (like when we went to
Space Camp together).

↓

↑
Nadia and me as salt and pepper shakers one
Halloween. How cute!

I can't wait to tell Carly. She's my best friend close by, right here and now. I just know she and Nadia are going to love each other!

The three of us are going to have so much fun together! We'll be like the Three Musketeers — I can't wait!

Nadia ↗   me ↑   ↶ Carly

At dinner I told Mom about Nadia's visit. I thought she'd be surprised, but she already knew. Which makes sense once you think about it. Nothing happens without parents first talking things out and making decisions. Kids are the last to know what's going on, even when whatever it is has to do with us.

At least everything's all set now. Mom's even already talked to my school about having Nadia sit in on my classes for the week.

Unfortunately Cleo was also at the dinner table. Trust my sister to turn something nice into something nasty.

That's totally unfair! If Amelia gets to have a friend visit, so do I! Or I should get to go stay with my old friends from our old place.

You're just jealous because none of your friends wants to see you — here or there. Do you even have a best friend?

Mom yelled at us to stop it. She said we should act our age instead of sticking out our tongues like babies. I can't help it. Being around Cleo is so INFURIATING I can't control myself. But I'd better. I don't want to get sucked into her stupid arguments when Nadia is here. I want everything to be perfect.

I wish I knew what makes Cleo SO annoying. Then I could develop an antidote for her, an anti-Cleo. I thought when she started high school she'd be better — or at least busier so I'd hardly see her — but she's worse. Now she's like exponential Cleo — Cleo x Cleo, bigger and louder than ever!

Carly's lucky. She has NO sisters, just two older brothers and they're both nice (and cute). She gets double goodness and I get Cleo. Yucch!

Marcus is 15 and one of the hottest — and coolest — boys I know. ↓

Malcom is 17 and gives Carly rides whenever she asks — lucky! ↓

At school the next day, I rushed up to Carly. I couldn't wait to tell her my news.

She could see something was up. ↓

What's going on? You look like you won the lottery. Has Cleo decided to move to Chicago to live with your dad?

Or did you win that art contest you entered? Did you happen to find a hundred dollar bill on the sidewalk?

"You're right," I said. "It is something great like winning the lottery or a contest."

"Well, what is it?"

You know Nadia, my old best friend in California before I moved here? I've told you about her — she's amazing! And now you'll get to meet her! She'll be here for a whole week! At my house and here in school, too!

You are excited. You're like a walking, talking exclamation point.

Sounds like you'll have a great time.

We'll have a great time! You're going to love her, I know it, and of course she'll love you. We can do all sorts of stuff together. It's gonna be so much FUN!

Strangely, Carly wasn't as excited as I thought she'd be. But then, she doesn't know Nadia — yet. Once she does, she'll see what a great week we're going to have, the best ever!

Carly may not have been excited about Nadia's visit, but she practically bounced out of her chair when Mr. Yegg, our social studies teacher, made his announcement.

Carly passed me a note.

Let's look at recipes tonight. We're definitely gonna win — I can taste it!

Normally I only enter drawing or writing contests. I mean, I like to bake. Who doesn't? But I'm not particularly good at it. Considering my mom and Cleo are both disasters in the kitchen, that shouldn't be a surprise. But I know Carly's a good cook, so I guess with her help I can make something delicious. Better yet, Nadia will be here and she's a GREAT baker. She even makes her own bread! The three of us together are bound to win! I felt so confident, I passed a note back to Carly.

And Nadia can help us! She's the queen of cookies, brownies, and fudge and a master of flaky pie crusts! I'll tell her to bring her recipes.

Carly crumpled up the note and didn't look at me. Did I hurt her feelings somehow? I didn't mean to, but sometimes you can insult people without knowing it.

At lunch I asked Carly if I'd said anything wrong.

"No," she sniffed. "I get it."

"Get what?" I sure didn't get it.

"I thought you wanted to enter the baking contest with me, but now I get it — you want to bake with Nadia."

I knew there was a misunderstanding!

"That's not it all. I want to bake with **both** of you."

"Hmmm," snorted Carly. "I'm not sure I want to do that. I don't even know Nadia."

"Just give her a chance," I begged. "I know once you meet her, you'll be best friends, too."

Carly just took a big bite of sandwich and didn't say anything else.

I took a bite of dry, dusty sandwich and didn't say anything either.

I felt like I'd put my foot in my mouth, not my lunch.

I needed to do something to get back on Carly's good side. So I made a chart of cooking do's and don'ts — that's the kind of thing she likes.

When I showed my Do's and Dont's to Carly, she laughed. Now things are back to normal. Phew! Amazing what a little drawing can do. And I'm sure once she actually meets Nadia, it'll all be a piece of cake — one we bake together.

We can even invent our own kind. →

Like instead of chocolate devil's food, why not cocoa friendship food? Sounds tastier!

Personally, I like devil's food.

That night I emailed Nadia about the bake-off.

"Bring ideas and recipes!" I wrote. She answered right away and said she's got lots of them. She's as excited as I am! I told her about Carly, Leah, Maya — she can't wait to meet everyone.

"And has Cleo improved with age?" she asked.

"Nope, the same old Cleo. Be prepared!" I warned.

"Anything else I should know about before I come?"

I couldn't think of anything. I didn't know I should have given her an entirely different warning.

watch out for falling rocks! ←

Look for jumping deer! ↓

Oh, no! School ahead — with kids walking in the way! →

That made me think. Road signs tell us to watch out for stuff. Wouldn't it be nice if there were signs like that in life so we'd be better prepared?

↑
Dangerous crossing—
dog poop ahead!

↑
Person in a bad
mood — do not talk
to or approach!

↑
Fart coming—
do not inhale!

↑
Boring book—
do not read
unless you
want a nap!

↑
Windbag ahead—
do not talk to unless
you want to hear details
about collecting jigsaw
puzzles!

↑
Shower at own risk—
all hot water
used up by
older sister!

Bad cook
at work! →

Do not eat
unless prepared
← for indigestion!

If there were really signs like that, I would have seen a big, bright flashing light.

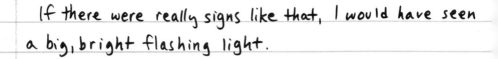

APPROACH WITH CAUTION GO SLOW!

But of course I didn't. Life isn't like that. So I just made my plans for the bake-off and told everyone about Nadia until finally, FINALLY, *FINALLY* it was time to pick her up at the airport.

I've always wanted to get off a plane and have someone with a sign waiting for me. →

So I did that for Nadia. She loved it! ↙

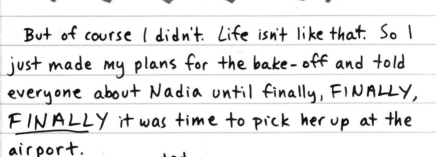

NADIA

I guess part of me had been worried that she'd changed somehow, but she was exactly the same. I mean, she was taller and her face was thinner, and she wore a bra, but she was still the same old Nadia. Easy to talk to, fun to be with, smart, sweet, and sensitive.

Maybe she'd been worried about me, too, because she said how great it was to see me again, like we'd never been apart.

It was a perfect day. Even Cleo was nice. She can be — sometimes.

she gave Nadia a big →
welcome hug.

Don't worry—I'll give you all the privacy you want. And I know you need the kitchen for baking, so I'll even limit my snacks.

Considering how Cleo loves to make big sandwiches, that was a nice offer.

The next day was Sunday, so we had all day
to relax together before school started. We
looked at recipes and talked a lot.

But there will still be some boring parts (like
dull lectures) and annoying parts (like P.E.).
I really owe Nadia as much fun as possible.

I tried to think of ways to make sure school would be entertaining. There's the bake-off at the end of the week, but what about all the days before Friday?

I could say it's my birthday and bring in cupcakes. I could ask the science teacher to demonstrate combustion again — explosions are always fun. I could bring in comics, bandes dessinées, for French. Comics in any language are great.

Or I could ask Carly to help me plan some fun things to do. I wanted to surprise Nadia so while she took a shower, I called Carly.

Amelia! I wondered if something happened to you. You haven't called all weekend.

Um, well, I've been kind of busy with Nadia.

She got here yesterday. That's what I'm calling about. I thought you might have some ideas how to make school fun for her.

Oh.   Then there was a long silence.

"Carly, did you hear me?" I finally asked.

"Yeees," she drawled like she didn't want to answer.

"Well, any suggestions?" I asked again.

"Nope, sorry. After all, I don't know Nadia at all so how would I know what's fun for her?"

She had a point. Maybe after meeting Nadia on Monday, Carly would get some ideas.

"I guess you're right. You'll see her tomorrow and then you'll know. It'll be great!"

"Yeah, sure, great." Carly didn't sound excited, but after all, she didn't know what there was to be excited about — yet! She'd find out!

Nadia came out of the shower just as I hung up.

who were you talking to?

Carly. She can't wait to meet you! You guys are going to love each other!

Sure.

Nadia didn't sound so excited, either. Tomorrow would change ← all that.

I was excited enough for the three of us on Monday morning. When I saw Carly, I rushed up to introduce Nadia. Only it didn't go at all like I expected.

It was awkward and uncomfortable and not perfec
at all. Nadia didn't know what to think.

You said Carly was great. She seems stuck-up, if you ask me.

No, really, she's not like that at all. Maybe she had a bad weekend. Or she has some big project due. She's really warm and smart and funny. Give her a chance. You'll see.

But Nadia didn't see. First we had science — without Carly — but my next class was English with Ms. Hanover. True, there wasn't a chance to talk during class, but before it began, I tried to say hi.

Carly wasn't exactly warm or smart or funny.

Can't talk now. I've got to finish this.

In fact, I could swear she was giving me the cold shoulder.

The next two classes were okay because Carly wasn't in them, but then came lunch — a complete disaster. Nadia tried, she really did, but Carly either disagreed or ignored her. I'd wanted to make school fun for Nadia, but now I'd settle for bearable. What happened to make everything turn out so badly?

"Carly!" I was shocked. "What's going on? Why are you being so mean?"

"I'm not mean," she snapped, sounding pretty mean. She gathered up her trash and left. Just like that.

"Wow!" Leah rolled her eyes. "She's really steamed. What did you do to put her off like that?"

"I didn't do anything!" I protested. "And neither did Nadia."

Nadia looked miserable.

That made me feel terrible, like it was all my fault. Which I guess in some way it was, since Carly was my friend. I had to fix things. Now!

I put my arm around Nadia. "Carly's just in a grouchy mood. Tomorrow will be much better, so don't worry. She definitely doesn't hate you." Even as I said it, I desperately hoped it was true.

Leah looked at me like I was crazy. She'd never seen Carly so "grouchy" before. But I have. When I've made her mad. An angry Carly can be pretty scary.

"Anyway," I changed the subject. "We need to talk about the bake-off. We have to decide what to enter."

That cheered Nadia up. She loves to bake. So does Leah. They were talking about kneading technique, milk chocolate vs. dark chocolate, all kinds of details that meant nothing to me. I'm not a very sophisticated baker. I just know the difference between:

burnt   and   not burnt

And to be honest, I like burnt cookies and brownies. Nothing like a little carbon crunch.

Leah's much more picky. "I want to make something super special, something no one else can make."

"I agree," Nadia nodded. "It's risky, but if you get it right, it'll be spectacular."

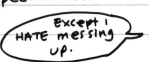

Except! HATE messing up.

I want it all to be perfect! I can't help it — I have HIGH standards, I admit it.

"I'm just the opposite," I admitted. "I don't mind making mistakes so long as I get another chance to make things right. Maybe that's because I do make so many mistakes. I guess I'm used to it."

It's one reason I like to write — you can always rewrite stuff to make it better. Too bad you can't rebake.

I wondered if I'd made a mistake with Carly, if I'd said or done anything to hurt her feelings. But Carly's always been clear — too clear — when I've done things before that upset her. She's NOT shy about telling me off.

Could I revise whatever made Carly mad? Too bad you can't redo things in life like you can in a notebook. You have to apologize and start fresh. Only I didn't know what I should apologize for.

My next class after lunch was social studies, another class with Carly. I didn't know how to make things better with her and I certainly didn't want to make things worse for Nadia, so this time I didn't even try to talk to Carly. I just introduced Nadia to Mr. Yegg, and we sat down together.

We're supposed to be studying Japan under the shoguns (same as Nadia at her school), but Mr. Yegg wanted to talk about baking.

Class, before we get to our samurai simulation, I wanted to talk a little bit about the bake-off from a historical point of view.

Have you ever wondered who invented baking? Who figured out that yeast makes dough rise? Who invented the chocolate chip cookie? Are there cookies in Japan or are they distinctly American?

I never thought about whether baked goods were part of our national culture, but maybe they are. After all, there's the expression, "As American as apple pie." I suppose the French equivalent would be "As French as croissants." For Italy, "As Italian as pizza." For Mexico, "As Mexican as tortillas."

Thinking about it, I was getting hungry even though we'd just had lunch.

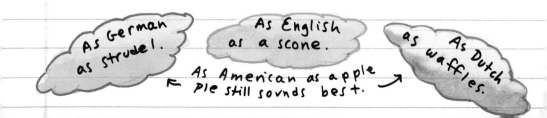

As German as strudel.

As English as a scone.

As Dutch as waffles.

← As American as apple pie still sounds best. →

For extra credit Mr. Yegg said we can write a page about the history of one particularly American bakery item, like buttermilk biscuits or cornbread. Then we'll get extra EXTRA credit if we bake enough of that item for the whole class to taste, plus give an oral report on it.

Nadia raised her hand.

I know I'm just visiting and not really in this class, but can I do a report on Parker House rolls? It's a great story!

Of course Mr. Yegg said yes — the more food for us to eat, the better! I'm proud of Nadia and I know she'll bake delicious rolls, whatever a Parker House roll is. I glanced at Carly. I thought now she'd see how great Nadia is, but she didn't look impressed. She looked angry.

In fact she looked so mad, I was afraid to go up to her after class or even after school.

Normally we walk home together but she wasn't waiting in the usual place. I was actually relieved not to see her. I didn't want a fight. I just wanted to have fun with Nadia.

Parker house rolls were invented at the Parker House hotel in Boston in the 19th century. It's where Boston cream pie was invented.

How do you know all this?

We stayed at the hotel once — it's still there, the oldest hotel in the U.S. A lot of famous people used to meet there for a club, poets and writers.

Like Ralph Waldo Emerson and Henry Wadsworth Longfellow.

Never heard of them. Did everyone have three names in those days?

It was a classic Nadia conversation. She's always full of these interesting tidbits of information. She should be on a game show.

For a while, being with Nadia was enough. I could forget how angry Carly seemed. But in the back of my head, a tiny voice kept reminding me.

Was that the reason? I had to find out. While Nadia was busy writing her report on rolls, I called Carly.

I felt terrible. I hadn't ignored her on purpose, but somehow saying that wasn't enough.

"Look, Carly, I'm sorry. I thought you and Nadia would be friends, but you haven't been welcoming. I couldn't abandon her."

If I thought Carly's voice was cold before, now it was positively frozen.

"Why would I be friends with her? Just because you are? I think she's a little teacher's pet — and she's not even really a student here! How pathetic is that?"

I could feel my cheeks go red and hot. "She's not like that!" I yelled. "It was brave of her to talk in class like she did today. I think it's great she wants to do work even without getting credit. And the Carly I thought I knew would think so, too."

There was a long pause. I tried to think of the right thing to say, but my mind was a blank.

which door to pick?
↓

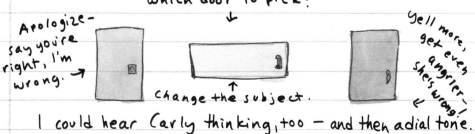

Apologize — say you're right, I'm wrong. →

change the subject. ↑

Yell more, get even angrier — she's wrong! ←

I could hear Carly thinking, too — and then a dial tone.

CARLY HUNG UP ON ME!

No one's ever hung up on me before — it felt AWFUL!
I was so upset, I was shaking. I wanted to call her back,
but I couldn't. I just stared at the phone like it was
poison or something.

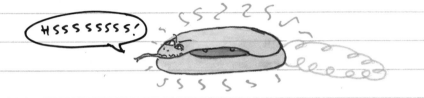

HSSSSSSSS!

I didn't want Nadia to see me like that. I didn't
want her to have any idea what Carly said about her.
So I sat at the kitchen table and took deep breaths,
trying to calm down.

Cleo came in for her usual sandwich.

"You're not baking yet, are you?" she
asked. "I'll make a snack later if you are."

"No, go ahead," I said. I was impressed
she'd actually bothered to ask. Sometimes
Cleo can surprise me that way.

"Is something the matter?" she
asked. She was piling pickles, lettuce,
tomatoes, cheese, and turkey on bread.

She was busy with her sandwich, but she still somehow noticed something was wrong. That surprised me even more.

So I blurted out what had happened.

"Wow," said Cleo between big bites of sandwich. "That's tough. Carly sounds really mad."

"Thanks for the cliché, Cleo," I said. "I don't buy it. Why can't they just get along? They don't have to be friends, but they can be friendly, can't they?"

"Just because you're friends with each of them, doesn't automatically mean they'll like each other. And chances are, they won't, because you get in the way." Cleo chomped loudly.

"I do not! I'm trying to bring them together!" The more Cleo explained, the less everything made sense.

"C'mon, Amelia! Try seeing it from Carly's point of view. You shove this stranger in her face, tell her Nadia's her new friend, and P.S. you'll be spending all your time with Nadia for a week, so Carly'd better like her."

When Cleo put it like that, it sounded terrible.

It reminded me of when we were little and Mom had a friend visit who happened to have a kid my age. ↓

This is Felicity. You'll have a wonderful time together.

You're the same age — you have so much in common! Isn't that amazing!

I always felt like saying, "Yeah, me and about a zillion other kids. That doesn't make us instant friends."

I got it. I really did.

But I still think Carly could have talked to me if she was annoyed instead of acting so mean. After all, none of this was Nadia's fault. She was an innocent bystander. And was it really that ridiculous for me to imagine the two of them could be friends? Carly didn't even give Nadia a chance.

"So what do I do to fix this mess?" I asked Cleo.

"Talk to Carly. Apologize. Tell her you understand. But you also need to be prepared."

"Prepared for what?" She made it sound like I was facing a pit of snakes or bubbling quicksand."

Sometimes finding your way through a friendship feels like that.

Burble, burble

SSSSSSS SSSSS S

"Prepared for Carly and Nadia simply not liking each other. It's hard when your friends don't get along. But it happens. And it's _your_ job to make it work with each one of them."

I put my head down on the kitchen table. It sounded exhausting. Why is it so much work sometimes to be a friend? →

Just then Nadia came into the kitchen, grinning. Glad somebody's happy.

"I'm finished!" she said, waving a piece of paper. "I've done my report on Parker House rolls. Now can we bake some?"

That sounded like a great idea. Everything's all right when there's the smell of fresh-baked bread.

Things that turn any bad mood into an instant good mood

cookies fresh from the oven

pajamas warm from the dryer

a purring cat

bare feet on sun-warmed grass

a hug from someone you love

hot cocoa

I felt so much better with a mouthful of fluffy, hot roll that I decided to call Carly back.

First I told Nadia what was going on, what Cleo thought, and how I was going to fix things.

Except Nadia didn't respond the way I thought she would. I thought she'd say yes, call Carly, if you tell her how much I want to be her friend, maybe she'll give me a chance.

She didn't.

The soft roll turned into hard rock in my stomach. Could it get any worse? Now Nadia doesn't like Carly and I'm the one stuck in between the two of them.

It was just like Cleo had warned me. This was supposed to be a great week, a perfect week, and it was turning into a perfect nightmare.

So I didn't call Carly. I couldn't with Nadia right there. And now it wasn't exactly friendly between us. It was cold and awkward. How did this happen? I used to have two best friends and now it looks like I have none.

I lay in bed thinking about how to fix things while Nadia watched a movie with Cleo — with Cleo!

↓

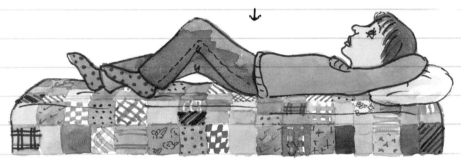

I wanted to call Carly to get her advice or write to Nadia the way I always do with my worst problems. But this time I couldn't, because they were both part of the problem.

I wasn't getting any ideas, so I decided to write a story in my notebook. That always makes me feel better, and at least I end up with something — a story.

FIX-IT

There was a girl who was a genius at fixing things. She could make a broken piggy bank look like new. She could sew loose buttons on shirts. She knew how to patch a bicycle tire or a roof. She was as handy with a hammer as with a needle and thread.

People came from all over asking her to fix things. Some had fancy watches. Others had complicated machines with lots of gears and switches. One woman wanted her to fix her sick cat.

The girl took care of all of them, even the cat. She was proud of all her achievements and was sure there was nothing she couldn't repair.

Look at me — I'm just like new!

I can do it!

No matter what!

Until one day three brothers came into her fix-it shop. They all looked very sad.

"You must have broken something very valuable," the girl said.

"We have," answered the oldest brother. "Each of us has a different problem. We've tried our best to make things whole again, but none of us has succeeded. We hope you can."

broken bits waiting to be made whole
↓

"Of course I can," the girl assured them. "Show me what's broken."

The oldest boy told her how he'd lied to his best friend and now the friend couldn't believe him about anything important. "I've broken his trust," said the boy.

The girl frowned. "I can't fix that."

"Can you help me then?" asked the middle boy. He told her how he loved a girl and she'd loved him until she saw him kissing another girl. "I didn't mean anything, really. It was a stupid mistake! But now I've broken her heart," said the boy.

The girl shook her head. "No amount of tape or glue can fix that, and I can't, either."

"Then there's not much hope for me, is there?" asked the youngest boy. He described how he'd argued with his best friend and though he was very sorry, his friend couldn't forgive him for the mean things he'd said. "I've broken our friendship. Please help me fix it," begged the boy.

The girl sighed. "I'm sorry. I can't help any of you. Only you can fix those things, not anybody else. But you've given me something."

"You've shown me that not everything can be fixed with a little oil or a few stitches. There's only one tool I can think of to help you."

"What is it?" asked the brothers.

"Words. You need to find the right words to mend a trust, a heart, a friendship. And only you can know which words are the right ones."

The boys saw what she meant and went home to fix their broken pieces. Whether they found the right words or not, I don't know. But the girl had found a new tool to add to her collection — a notebook. Every night after she finished her repairs, she wrote in her notebook, looking for the right words for herself.

I don't know why, but I always feel better after I write down what I'm feeling.

It's kind of like a brain massage or a whole brain tonic.

The End

After I finished the story, I knew what I had to do. No matter what Nadia said, I had to talk to Carly. And no matter what Carly said, I had to talk to Nadia. But first, I had to talk to myself. I had to be honest and admit that when I'd expected Carly and Nadia to be instant best friends, I hadn't been thinking about them.

I'd been thinking about me. I'd been selfish. And insensitive. I had to admit to Carly and Nadia what I'd done wrong, ask them to forgive me, and start all over again with what they wanted.

It was the only thing I could think of. It had to work.

When Nadia came to bed, I told her I was sorry about what happened with Carly.

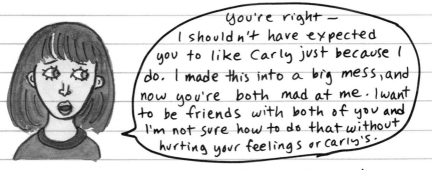

You're right — I shouldn't have expected you to like Carly just because I do. I made this into a big mess, and now you're both mad at me. I want to be friends with both of you and I'm not sure how to do that without hurting your feelings or Carly's.

There was a long silence. It seemed even longer because it was dark — a long, thick, dark, heavy silence.

I was afraid to say anything else and I thought Nadia had given up on me and fallen asleep. But she hadn't. I heard her sigh.

"It's okay, Amelia," she finally said. "You're in a tough situation, the kind of problem you would write to me about on a postcard. Only now I'm part of the problem."

"I thought the same thing!" I said. "I've missed asking for your advice — and getting it."

So now I'm imagining what advice I would give you if I weren't one of the friends you were caught between.

There was another silence, shorter this time and not so heavy.

"I don't know, Amelia. It's hard for me to say. Carly and I just don't get along. She clearly doesn't like me and I don't like her. That doesn't mean we can't be your friends, but it does mean you can't spend time with us together. You have to choose."

"That's impossible!" I said, "How can I choose?"

"I don't mean you have to stop being friends with Carly while I'm here, but at least don't eat lunch with her. Please? It's SO unpleasant!"

I sighed. Nadia was right. It was terrible.

"Okay, but give me a chance to talk to Carly about it. I need her to understand it's not forever, just for while you're here."

"Thanks!" Nadia said. "I feel much better."

"Me too," I agreed. Still, I worried about Carly. She might get really mad at me. Then what would I do?

All I could do was talk to her, try to use my words to fix things, and hope for the best.

If I could get to sleep and tomorrow ever came.

I stared into the darkness for a long time. What if Carly decided I wasn't worth it, she didn't want to be my best friend anymore?

It was one of those nights where you only know that you finally fell asleep because you wake up. I didn't feel rested at all. At least Nadia was in a good mood. She had her Parker House rolls and report ready to bring to school. I hoped the snack would put everyone in a good mood, especially Carly.

At lunch Nadia sat with Leah while I talked to Carly.

What happened to Little Miss Perfect?

You mean Nadia? She's not perfect.

She seems to think so.

Look, Carly, that's what I wanted to talk to you about, this whole Nadia thing.

"Yeah, what about it?" Carly snapped.

"I'm sorry!" I blurted out. "I'm sorry I thought you'd like her just because I do. But she is my friend and she's staying with me this week, so I have to spend time with her." I swallowed the lump in my throat. "That doesn't mean you have to be with her, though. Maybe the rest of the week I should eat lunch with just Nadia. We'll have the rest of the year to eat lunch together."

Carly glared. "You're right that you shouldn't have assumed we'd be best buddies, but you're wrong to dump me to have lunch with Nadia. There's no reason we can't all eat together. I may not like Nadia, but I can be perfectly civil to her."

"You weren't yesterday!" I said.

"That was before you apologized. Now that you have, I promise I'll behave."

"Really?" I pressed.

"Really!" Carly insisted.

I had to trust her. What choice did I have? But since Nadia looked happy with Leah, I decided we'd start group lunches tomorrow.

← For now I tried to have a normal conversation with Carly, but it all felt clumsy and awkward. I wanted to go back to how we used to be. Had I ruined everything?

BRRRRING! The bell rang and we all headed to Social Studies together. Nadia seemed happy after talking to Leah. Carly was quiet. So was I.

Mr. Yegg was thrilled to see Nadia with her rolls. They definitely put _him_ in a good mood.

Nadia, let's start class with your rolls. Pass them around and we'll listen to your report.

Nadia handed out the rolls along with the recipe and told stories about the Parker House Hotel. She did a great job.

PARKER HOUSE ROLLS

This recipe works best if you have a large stand mixer → If you don't, beat the dough really well as you add flour. Nobody will ever make these as light and fluffy as my grandma, but every year, I try!

1 c. whole milk	1/2 c. butter, melted	1/2 c. sugar	4 1/2 - 5 c. flour
2 pkg. dry yeast	1/4 tsp. salt	2 eggs	more melted butter

Warm milk in a small saucepan over low heat. Mix 1/3 of milk with yeast in a small bowl and let sit until bubbly, about 15 minutes. Put rest of milk into large bowl, add melted butter, salt, and sugar. Beat until sugar is dissolved. Add beaten eggs and bubbly yeast mixture. Add flour 1/4 cup at a time, using large stand mixer to beat at high speed. It should take 5 minutes to really beat flour well. When dough is too stiff to beat, stir in remaining flour by hand (if needed), enough to make a soft dough. Turn out onto a floured board and knead 5 minutes, until smooth and satiny. Place dough in greased bowl, turning over to grease both sides. Cover with a towel and let rise in a warm place until doubled in size, about 1 hour. Punch down dough and roll out onto floured board to 1/2" thick. Cut with 3" round cookie cutter (or use upside-down glass). Brush each roll with butter and fold in half. Pinch edge lightly so doesn't unfold as it bakes. Place in 2 greased 9" or 13" pans, cover with a towel, and let rise again in warm place until doubled in size, about 45 minutes. Bake at 350° for 20-25 minutes, until golden brown. Remove from pan and immediately brush with fresh melted butter. Now eat! Deee-licious!

I glanced at Carly. She looked interested — and she'd eaten all her roll.

After class Carly came up to us. "Nice job, Nadia," she said. "And you're a good baker. That roll was tasty!"

"Thanks!" Nadia's eyes sparkled like they do when she's really happy. "And I'm sorry I've caused problems between you and Amelia. Don't worry — I'll be gone in a few days. You too, Amelia — stop looking so miserable because I'm here."

"What? I'm glad you're here! I'm just worried, that's all."

"Stop worrying," Carly said.

"Stop worrying," Nadia echoed.

I was so confused I didn't know what to say, but the bell rang and we had to hurry or be late to French.

After school Carly wasn't at our usual place. That seemed like a bad sign. Nadia didn't think so.

"Didn't you tell her at lunch that you needed to spend time with me? She's just giving you that time. Really, it's nice of her."

"I hope you're right," I said.

She was and she wasn't. As soon as we got home, Carly called.

"What did Carly say?" Nadia wanted to know. I wanted to lie, but I didn't. I told her the choice Carly had given me.

"How can I do that?" I asked. "You're both my best friend. I don't want to hurt either of you."

"Look," said Nadia. "I'll make it easy on you — on ONE condition. I'm happy to bake with Leah. She already asked me, so I know she'll agree."

"Really?! You wouldn't mind?" I was so relieved, I felt like I'd just aced a horrible final exam. Then I remembered something she'd said. "Um ... what's the one condition?"

"I get to use our favorite recipe, the one for chocolate chip peppermint cookies. You and Carly have to bake something else."

It seemed like such a small condition, I should have been thrilled. But that's also Carly's favorite recipe. What if she insisted we bake them? I decided I would deal with that problem if it happened — later. At least the impossible choice had been taken care of.

"Thanks, Nadia!" I hugged her. "You're the best!"

"Remember that," she said. "I'm your <u>best</u> best friend."

And right then, she definitely was.

I called Carly back and told her I'd be baking with her, not Nadia. I could tell she was happy I'd chosen her — and that I'd decided so quickly.

"Guess that makes me your <u>best</u> best friend, huh?" she said.

"Yeah!" I squeaked. It was kind of true, in a way, maybe not that second, but still... I had to change the subject. "What should we make? How about some kind of pie? Mr. Yegg is big on pies."

"That's a good idea," she said.

"Phew!!" I thought.

Carly's going to ask her mom for a good pie recipe.

So many to choose from!

That was close! The pie suggestion worked —
Carly didn't even mention cookies. Yet. I wondered
if I'd survive this week. I had thought it would be so
much fun, but it was like walking through a minefield.
Avoid these dangers — step carefully!

GRRR

liver and onions—
P.U.!

← mean dogs

gum on
your shoe

Come with
me!

evil rats →

exploding
toilets

abducting
aliens

BZZZZ₂

Sniff!
Is that
me?

← hungry mosquitos

smelly
armpits

you're
late!

Jell-o with mystery
lumps inside

poison oak—
dangerous
itching
ahead!

overdue
library
books

Hi!

GASP!

bad breath

fighting friends

The next day at school, the four of us had lunch together,
Leah, Nadia, Carly, and me. We talked about baking and how
to make something that stands out from the crowd.

Leah said there are two ways to go — make something
classic that everyone loves and do a brilliant job. Or
figure out an odd combination that sounds like it wouldn't
taste good together, but turns out to be surprisingly
scrumptuous.

Like pineapple
on pizza...

...or brownies
with curry powder...

...or pumpkin
butterscotch
bars...

...or chocolate
and peanut butter — a brilliant combination!

That seemed risky. You could end up with something gross,
like peanut butter and ketchup. Cleo used to like that!
Just because you like two things separately doesn't mean
they'll go well together.

Nadia disagreed. She said you have to be creative and
try new things. And some things are sure to taste great —
like peppermint.

Peppermint carrot cake? Peppermint oatmeal cookies?
I wasn't so sure. Carly said it's not peppermint, but
chocolate that makes everything taste better.

I wasn't sure about that either. Chocolate apple pie? Chocolate prune danish? Yucch!

That made me think. Mixing friends can be like mixing ingredients. Coconut doesn't go with tomato, mint doesn't go with lemon. That was what happened with Carly and Nadia — two great friends who don't go together at all! If I think about them like butterscotch and lemon, it makes sense!

Which I guess is why I need to try to keep them apart. At least in the kitchen.

I showed Carly the recipes I'd brought, none of which had creative ingredients. Chocolate mousse, pumpkin cheesecake, and classic apple pie.

Her recipes were the opposite kind — the sort with unexpected surprise ingredients like ginger or pineapple extract.

We were so different, for a second I wondered if we mixed well together. Maybe she wasn't really my best friend.

Then I realized how silly I was being. Carly's a better cook, that's all.

We both agreed on one of her recipes — pear pie with gruyere crust. Gruyere is a kind of cheese. Sounds strange, but Carly insists it's yummy.

lemon merengue   chocolate cream   pecan   pumpkin
strawberry

I figured it was a good choice even though it sounded ~~weird weird~~ weird (like this word!) because I like making pies. And I love eating them.

After school, Nadia went home with Leah to bake and I went home with Carly.

And somehow being in the cozy kitchen, stirring and measuring, rolling out dough and slicing pears, we were back to being our old selves again, back to being simply best friends.

It was great.

We joked and laughed like nothing had ever been wrong.

The best part was once we'd finished. We rolled out the extra pie crust and made honey pies with the scraps. We couldn't taste the finished pear pie since we had to enter it into the bake-off, but at least we could eat the honey pies — yum!

How to make a honey pie: roll out the extra dough, smear with butter, cinnamon, and sugar. Fold over into a pocket. Press edges with a fork to seal. Bake and eat while warm!

BAKE-

Mama!

The day of the contest, the whole school smelled great! Not like rubber balls and white board markers, but like chocolate, cinnamon, licorice. Everything looked delicious. I wished I was one of the judges so I could taste it all. Lucky Mr. Yegg and Ms. Li got that job.

"Your pear pie looks amazing!" Nadia said. "I always have problems getting the crust to look pretty."

"Thanks," said Carly. She deserved all the credit for how well our pie turned out. If I'd made it alone, it would have been a Frankenstein pie.

"Your cookies smell wonderful," Carly said. "That's my favorite recipe, too."

I stared at them. If I didn't know better, I'd say they were acting like friends. Maybe it was all the good smells they were breathing in.

OFF! HATSOFF TO THE BAKERS!

Another cookie factoid: Tollhouse cookies were actually invented in a tollhouse. Ruth Wakefield and her husband ran a lodge in an old tollhouse near Boston. She was trying for something else entirely when she made the first chocolate chip cookie — a brilliant mistake!

There were so many desserts to choose from, I didn't think we had much chance of winning. So I wasn't too disappointed when Eli won first prize for his dark chocolate mousse.

"We could have made that," Carly whispered to me. "I should have listened to you — classic beats oddball every time."

"Not every time. And then we wouldn't have made honey pie — that was worth more than a prize."

"Maybe," Carly said. "But I like to win."

I laughed. "I'd rather eat!" Now that the judging was over, it was a regular bake sale. I bought slices of pie for all of us to try. Yummy!

mmm mmmm mmm mmm mmm mmm mmm!

We each bought something different and traded tastes.
It was a bakery feast — and a sweet way for
Nadia to end her visit.

The next day we drove her to the airport.
"It wasn't what I expected, but I loved having
you here," I said. "You'll always be my best
friend, no matter what!"
"Yeah." Nadia smiled. "You've proven that!
It's cool that we can grow and change and still
be friends. I've outgrown other friends — not
you." She hugged me. "Next time you come
see me. Maybe that'll be easier."
I nodded. Somehow I imagine it won't be,
but it won't matter, not one bit. We'll deal
with it.

I have faith we'll stay friends. →

No matter what. ←

Then Carly came over and it was like Nadia had never been here. No more tension, no more ruffled feathers, just me and Carly, best friends, baking together.

This time we made our favorite cookies, even better than honey pie.

And that's what makes true best friends.

MORE

Amelia's Notebooks

write on!

I've written ~~22~~ 23 notebooks! which is your favorite?

Read on!

I wish I could forget them!

← Pssst! Did you hear the one about Mr. L?

The good, the bad, and the totally freaky!

Carly's favorite so far!

Plus all these from elementary school!

The first and original!

Still my favorite!

There's lots more info and fun stuff at marissamoss.com and KIDS.simonandschuster.com. Even a real Amelia movie!